D1561634

A High School Guide to Chemistry

Told through a collection of short stories.

Bhavish Dinakar

Bhavish Dinakar

ISBN: 1530650577
ISBN-13: 978-1530650576

DEDICATION

To the Periodic Table of Elements.

CONTENTS

Chapter 1

ENTHALPY OF FORMATION

Dr. Hofbrincl had just drunk some 5-hour Energy, and he was now feeling quite energetic.

"I'm feeling very energetic," he said.

"That's great!" exclaimed his wife, Mrs. Hofbrincl. "Now you can use that energy to mow the front lawn and to wash the dishes!"

"Eh," Dr. Hofbrincl replied.

He decided that he would go outside and take a walk to use up his extra energy. He could have decided to go for a run instead, but chose not to because he was lazy.

Dr. Hofbrincl, by the way, is the protagonist of the story, if you hadn't noticed.

As he was walking, he looked around, amazed at all of the sights around him. He saw a bird land on a tree branch, a gust of wind swirling some leaves, and his neighbor walking a dog.

"That bird looks so wonderful! So do those leaves! And wait, why does that man have a hairy baby on a leash?"

As he turned the corner, he arrived at Main Street, which was, unsurprisingly, the main street in his town. He saw many billboards with messages such as "Free Sandwiches With Purchase" and "This Restaurant Will Give You Food Poisoning." However, there was one sign that struck his fancy: "Invest Your Extra Energy in the Enthalpy Bank."

Invest my extra energy??? he thought. That's right, he had three question marks in his head.

I do have a lot of extra energy. I might as well keep it in this bank.

Upon realizing that he had a lot of extra energy, he decided to pay a visit to the bank.

Now that we have the introduction to the story out of the way, we can actually begin the part that applies to chemistry. Unless you don't want to learn about chemistry, in which case you should read the next paragraph in order to delay learning about chemistry as long as possible. If you want to learn about chemistry, then skip the next paragraph.

At this point, Dr. Hofbrincl realized that his shoes were untied. *Oh, no!* he thought. *If my shoes are untied, then there is a greater probability that I will slip and fall at some point.* Therefore, he decided to tie his shoes. As he tied his shoes, he remembered all the colors of the rainbow: red, orange, yellow, green, blue, indigo, violet. Then, he counted to ten: 1, 2, 3, 4, 5, 6, 7, 8, 9, 10. Finally, he stopped delaying the story for no reason and entered the Bank of Enthalpy.

"Hi," he said to the teller as he approached the desk. "I have some extra energy, and I'd like to invest it."

"That's great!" said the teller, who's name coincidentally also happened to be Teller. "What would you like to do with your energy? At this location, we offer heat, work, and bonds."

"Well, I already have a lot of heat from all this vigorous walking I've been doing, and I guess you could also consider my working out to be work. So I guess I'll choose a bond, Teller."

"Please, call me Tell," said Tell the teller.

"So which bond can I buy?" Dr. Hofbrincl asked.

"I'm sorry, sir, but you can't buy bonds. You can only break them or form them. You have to pay energy to break a bond, and you get energy returned to you when a bond is formed. It costs more to break a double-bond, and even more to break a triple-bond. And if you have exactly .007 kJ of energy, then we call that a James Bond."

"So if I have an extra 2000 J of energy right now, I can use it to break a bond? And then later, when the bond forms again, I'll get my energy back?" asked Dr. Hofbrincl.

"Unfortunately, we don't accept joules of energy, only kilojoules. You'll have to convert your energy, and remember to take significant figures into account."

"Wow, that's really annoying. At least I have to convert it only once, instead of for a whole year, like high school IB students have to do in their Chemistry classes. Well anyways, I guess I have 2 kJ to invest. So now when I invest my 2 kJ in the Enthalpy Bank, I'll get the energy back with interest when I come back later?"

"Unfortunately, no. Recently, the government passed a law called the Law of Conservation of Energy stating that energy can neither be created nor destroyed. It's quite bureaucratic, really," said Tell the teller.

Dr. Hofbrincl thought the matter over in his head. Except he wasn't thinking about matter, but energy. He decided that even though he didn't gain anything, he would still invest the energy because he wasn't very good at making rational decisions.

Suddenly, the temperature of the room dropped. Dr. Hofbrincl felt very chilly.

"Wow, it's like 10 degrees Celsius colder in here now," he said.

"Actually, you mean 10 Celsius degrees, not 10 degrees Celsius," said Tell. "Anyways, the reason it's colder is because you broke a bond, which is an endothermic process. When another bond forms, the room will heat up again."

"You should try out air conditioning instead," suggested Dr. Hofbrincl. "It works quite well."

"We wanted to, but it is much too expensive," said Tell. "Well, thank you for coming and investing in the Bank of Enthalpy."

As Dr. Hofbrincl walked home, he realized that he was out 2000 J of energy. He began feeling very drowsy, and soon his eyes were shutting – he needed something to keep him awake, and fast! He saw a nearby coffee shop and thought that coffee would wake him up.

"Excuse me, ma'am. Can I have some coffee?"

"I'm sorry, sir, but we're all out."

He kept trudging on. He saw a store selling Gatorade and walked through the front door.

"Don't bother coming in here. We're all sold out of Gatorade."

Tired and helpless, he realized that he wasn't going to be able to make it back to his house. Instead, he turned around and started crawling, slowly but steadily, back to the Bank of Enthalpy.

"I need my energy," he hissed. "My ... precious ... energy."

Dr. Hofbrincl could take it no longer. Gasping for breath, he grasped the door handle and went inside, grappling with the other customers to get to the teller's desk.

"Tell!" he yelled. "Quick! I need more energy right now!"

"Right away, sir," replied Tell as he went to get the energy. "Because you want energy, we must form a bond, which is an exothermic process. This means that ...."

"There's no time for your Chemistry lessons, Tell! Hurry up! I could die any minute now!"

"All right, here you go," said Tell as he handed Dr. Hofbrincl 1900 J of energy.

"1900 Joules? I thought I had invested 2000 J," said Dr. Hofbrincl.

"That is correct," said Tell. "However, whenever we convert energy, some of it is lost to the surroundings as heat."

"Oh, that's unfortunate. On the bright side, I guess it helps keep the room warm."

After a long day of breaking and forming bonds, Dr. Hofbrincl decided that he was done for the day. He walked back to his house and took a very long nap.

Key points:

1. Breaking a bond is endothermic and forming a bond is exothermic. Endothermic means the enthalpy change is positive and that it requires energy from the surroundings. Exothermic means that the enthalpy change is negative and that it releases energy to the surroundings.

2. Double-bonds and triple-bonds contain more energy than single-bonds. The greater the number of bonds formed, the greater the energy required to break them.

3. The enthalpy of formation is the amount of energy you must add in order to form the substance from the most stable states of its elements.

4. When performing enthalpy of formation calculations, simply add up the total energy on the left side of the equation, and add up the total energy on the right side of the equation. If you put in more energy breaking bonds than you get forming bonds, then the total enthalpy change is positive. If you get more energy back by forming bonds than you have to spend to break them, then the enthalpy change is negative.

Chapter 2

PLATING

After he woke up from his nap, Dr. Hofbrincl decided that he was going to spend the evening lying on his couch watching TV. He had hoped that he could watch college football, but the TV remote was on the other side of the room, and it would require way too much effort for him to go and retrieve it. Therefore, he decided that the TV channel he was currently watching was fine. It was the daily news channel.

"Attention, everyone. There has been a huge disaster in the Iron Sulfate factory. It appears that there has been a leak in the factory, and it has now contaminated Lake Hydroxicacid," said the news reporter.

"Gosh darn," exclaimed Dr. Hofbrincl as he slapped his knee in disappointment. He had wanted to go sailing that weekend in Lake Hydroxicacid, a local lake. Unfortunately, it appeared that the lake was now poisoned with some runoff from the Iron Sulfate factory. This meant his sailing plans were ruined because of the leak. He also did not know how to sail or own a boat, so that was also a problem.

"And now," continued the reporter, "some words from our sponsors."

Well, you win some, you lose some, thought Dr. Hofbrincl. He had already forgotten about his sailing plans, and was thinking of places he could try skydiving instead.

Suddenly, he noticed that the TV was showing the trailer for the new Iron Man movie.

"Iron Man! That's awesome," he exclaimed. He had always wanted to be as cool as Iron Man ever since he was a small child. He thought it was so cool how a man could build his own superhero outfit instead of being born with superpowers. If only he could build his own Iron Man suit …

Wait, he thought. *I just got a raise at work. Why don't I just build one myself?*

Armed with a newly found vigor, he began gathering materials for his Iron Man suit. After a couple of hours hard at work, he found some toothpaste and a couple of Snickers bars.

This won't do, he thought. *Although those Snickers bars look good*. Dr. Hofbrincl then proceeded to eat both Snickers bars.

Then, he had a stroke of genius. Why should he bother building an Iron Man suit when he could just buy one instead?

Dr. Hofbrincl opened up his computer and opened up Internet Explorer. He began typing into the Bing search engine, his home page. Then, he realized that Google was much better than Bing, so he downloaded Google Chrome, and searched for an Iron Man suit on Google.

Wow! And it comes with free shipping! Dr. Hofbrincl was very excited about his Iron Man suit. In fact, he was so excited that he didn't do anything except wait around for his suit to come in the mail.

Days passed. Then weeks, months. Years. His wife began to get worried, and his boss tried to fire him, but could not get in contact with Dr. Hofbrincl to fire him, so he technically still received paychecks. He didn't eat, didn't sleep, and didn't move from his front doorstep.

Finally, the package arrived. He grabbed the box, tore it apart with his bare hands, and jumped into the suit.

Except there was only one problem.

The suit wasn't made of iron.

It was made of zinc.

Zinc.

His world came crashing down around him. His life, his dreams, his aspirations: they were all ruined. Ruined. Gone. His precious, precious Iron Man suit was really just zinc.

Zinc.

Well, these past three years have been a huge waste of time, he thought. *I guess it's now time to get rid of this godforsaken suit.*

He put the suit in his car, and drove to the nearest bridge. Then, he threw the suit off the bridge.

Finally, all of my misery is over. I can start my life anew.

The suit hit the surface of the water with a very satisfying "Thud." It slowly began sinking, deeper and deeper into Lake Hydroxicacid until Dr. Hofbrincl could barely see it anymore.

But then, something magical happened. Dr. Hofbrincl couldn't believe his eyes. He had to look away and look back multiple times to make sure that he wasn't hallucinating. Because all of a sudden, it appeared as if the suit had changed from being covered with zinc to being covered with iron.

Immediately, he jumped into Lake Hydroxicacid in order to rescue his precious, precious suit.

Thank God you're still here, he thought as he held up his suit, which had now suddenly become plated with iron. Although it was quite heavy, and he was having a hard time keeping afloat. Fortunately, he had brought a life jacket with him, which he used as a flotation device to prevent the suit from drowning.

Once he finally got back on dry land, he began examining the suit to make sure that it was really made of iron. And although he was absolutely positively certainly sure that it was made of zinc previously, it was clear that the suit was now made of iron.

Instead of wondering why the suit had become iron, Dr. Hofbrincl was just happy that he now had a fully functioning Iron Man suit. However, since he had thrown it in a lake, water had gotten into all of the wires, and the suit had lost all of its cool functions like flight and shooting awesome flame things.

Explanation

The reason why the suit turned from zinc to iron has to do with the leak from the Iron Sulfate factory (for the record, I have no idea if iron sulfate factories exist or not). When the iron sulfate went into Lake Hydroxiacid, it dissociated into iron ions and sulfate ions.

This meant that when the zinc suit was thrown into the lake, it began reacting with the iron and sulfate ions dissolved in the water. Since zinc is more reactive than iron, the zinc atoms became zinc ions and gave electrons to the iron ions in the water, which then attached themselves to the suit in order to form an iron layer outside. This is a process in which a zinc object becomes plated with iron.

This can be generalized by saying that if you dip a solid metal object into a solution with a metal ion that is less reactive than the substance the object is made out of, then the object will become plated by the metal that is in solution.

Key Points:

1. If you have a metal that is ionized and dissolved in solution, and another metal that is a solid, then the more reactive metal will become ionized and dissolved in solution, and the less reactive metal will become a solid.

2. Zinc is more reactive than iron.

3. You should try this at home with some paperclips (which are plated with zinc) and a common chemistry solution such as copper(II) sulfate. Since zinc is more reactive than copper, if you place the paperclips in the solution, they will become plated with copper.

4. Never go into a lake that has a bunch of iron sulfate dissolved in it.

Chapter 3

REDOX

"Redox! Redox! Get your redox here!"

Dr. Hofbrincl was driving back home from the movie theater when he saw a young chap holding a sign that was labeled "Redox."

"What is a Redox?" he said to himself, even though he was alone in the car and there was nobody else around him. He was tired and groggy after eating too much popcorn at the movie theater, and he wanted to go home and take a nap. However, he became slightly intrigued as to what this "Redox" shenanigan was.

He pulled up his car right next to the boy and rolled down the window.

"So are you selling tickets to some sort of rodeo about red oxen?" Dr. Hofbrincl asked.

"Actually, yes," said the boy. "Just kidding. No, we're not."

"Oh. So are you re-training old doctors?"

"Um…ya. Just kidding, again. No, we're not."

"You have a horrible sense of humor," said Dr. Hofbrincl.

"I know. It's almost as bad as your haircut," replied the boy.

"True, true," said Dr. Hofbrincl. "So what are you doing?"

The young boy pulled out a sheet of paper and began to read: "Hi, welcome to the Redox Corporation! My name is Insert Name Here, and I'm here to serve you today."

Dr. Hofbrincl was confused by this statement and raised one eyebrow in confusion, as he did not understand the matters present at hand.

"Oh, sorry," said the boy. "I should have inserted my actual name instead of saying Insert Name Here. Let's try that again."

The young boy pulled out a sheet of paper and began to read: "Hi, welcome to the Redox Corporation! My name is Duce, and I'm here to serve you today. We at the Redox Corporation love to promote synergy, core competency, innovative marketing strategies for a 21st century marketing base, and various other corporate buzzwords. Here, we would like to share with everyone the pleasure of being Oxidized."

Dr. Hofbrincl finally understood what the Redox Corporation was about.

"So is the Redox Corporation kind of like a spa?"

Duce nodded his head. "Exactly. Except not really. It's actually the complete opposite. But nice try."

"I do my best," Dr. Hofbrincl said.

"So, are you ready to be Oxidized?" asked Duce.

"I was born ready," said Dr. Hofbrincl. He was proud of his use of hyperbole, a skill which he had learned during his senior year of high school. This was the first and perhaps last time he had used skills he learned in his English class since he graduated. Clearly, literary analysis was a valuable usage of time.

"All right!" exclaimed Duce. "All you have to do is hand over $500, and we'll be ready to start."

"Okay." Dr. Hofbrincl rummaged around in his wallet to find $500. He never thought to question what he was getting into because he didn't really think about the future.

"All right, here's all the money I have with me. I only have $499. Will that be enough?"

"I'm sorry, no," replied Duce. "We at the Redox Corporation are very stringent about our money. That way, we can make as much of a profit as possible through the American capitalist system."

This news was unfortunate for Dr. Hofbrincl. Upon hearing that he could not be Oxidized, whatever that was, he was devastated. He was heartbroken. And above all, he was sad.

Fortunately, there was a nearby ATM. Dr. Hofbrincl got the extra dollar and returned to Duce's booth.

"I'm back!" he exclaimed. "I'm ready to be Oxidized! Let's go!"

He was super excited. This would be his first ever time being Oxidized! He imagined that in the future, he would tell his children of this moment, a moment in history that would never be forgotten.

"Good job," said Duce. "Now hand over the $500, and we'll begin."

Dr. Hofbrincl forked over the $500, which was incidentally his life savings, with a smile on his face and joy in his heart.

"I'm ready whenever you are," he said, waiting in anticipation.

"Um…" said Duce. "Actually, that's it. By giving me the $500 without anything in return, you've successfully been Oxidized!"

Dr. Hofbrincl was shocked. He had just consented to giving a random stranger, one who was named Duce for that matter, his life's savings and had gotten nothing in return. All that had happened was that he was now apparently "Oxidized," whatever that meant.

But at the same time, he was ecstatic. He had finally achieved his minute-long dream of being Oxidized! Now, he would have something to tell his wife and possibly future kids, or maybe even grandkids. He could already imagine himself sitting on an old rocking chair in his living room with his grandchildren on his knees, telling them about the time he had been Oxidized.

"Thank you for conducting business with the Redox Corporation. If this did not satisfy all of your needs, please fill out this survey so we know how to improve in the future," said Duce, who had gone back to reading from the sheet of paper.

"Um, I just have one question," said Dr. Hofbrincl. "What exactly does it mean to be Oxidized?"

"Let's see," said Duce, as he scanned the paper with his eyes, trying to find out what the Redox Corporation wanted him to say in response to this question. "Yes, found it! All right, here we go."

Duce then proceeded to read out the pre-written response he was given.

"This whole experience is an analogy for what happens with atoms during chemical reactions. In chemistry, a Redox Reaction means a reaction involving Reduction and Oxidation, hence the name. If an atom gains electrons, then its charge is lowered because electrons have a negative charge. Therefore, if it has more electrons, it will be Reduced. However, if an atom loses electrons in a chemical reaction, then it has a greater charge and will therefore be Oxidized. In our transaction, think of your $500 as electrons. When you gave the electrons to me, you were Oxidized because you gained a positive charge. However, I, Insert Name Here, am…"

Duce paused for a second, realizing his mistake. "Let's try that again," he said.

"However, I, Duce, was Reduced during this transaction because when you gave me the $500 worth of electrons, I gained a negative charge."

Duce finished reading the statement and looked up at Dr. Hofbrincl. Then, they both shared a moment of understanding.

"So I guess that's why my name is Duce," Duce said. "It's because I'm being Re-Duce-d. That's weird. I always wondered why the Redox Corporation made me change my name."

Dr. Hofbrincl was astounded. "So is everyone who works at the Redox Corporation named Duce?" he asked

"Actually, yes," replied Duce. "And I'm not even joking this time. It's kind of weird, actually."

"In that case," said Dr. Hofbrincl, "why don't they just replace the Insert Name Here in the script with Duce?"

"You know what, that's actually kind of a good idea," said Duce. "You are a very wise man."

"Tell me something I don't know," said Dr. Hofbrincl. "Anyways, it was great conducting business with you. Although I am now out $500, and get nothing in return. My life savings are all gone, and I will probably have nothing to eat for dinner."

Duce smiled at Dr. Hofbrincl in sympathy.

"Look on the bright side. Now you don't have to walk around with $500 on you all the time. You'll weigh less, so you'll be able to move more quickly. There's also less harm in you getting mugged, because you can truthfully say that you have no money on you if you get attacked," suggested Duce.

"I guess that's true," said Dr. Hofbrincl. "I do weigh a lot. And I do hate getting mugged. I guess I would rather my money go to giant profit-loving capitalism-exploiting corporations than socioeconomically disadvantaged people who actually need it."

The two men, now good friends, parted ways. Dr. Hofbrincl, now happy and content with his life choices, drove back to his home and took a well-deserved nap.

Chapter 4

MASS SPECTROMETER

One day, Dr. Hofbrincl decided that he was getting out of shape. Ever since he had been a small child, he had never been one for exercise, preferring to play video games and eat lots of cupcakes instead. However, he realized that he had had enough of this lifestyle of sitting around and wasting away. He decided he would do something that nobody would ever expect him to: run the city marathon - an ultimate testament to his strength and endurance as an athlete.

"What a great idea!" Mrs. Hofbrincl exclaimed. "This way, you will finally get some exercise for once in your life." She then proceeded to give Dr. Hofbrincl a chocolate cake, which was his daily afternoon snack.

"Then it's settled," said Dr. Hofbrincl. "As soon as I finish this slice of cake, I'm going to begin my training. I will not sleep, I will not eat, I will not rest until I have won the marathon.

After he finished eating his piece of cake, he decided to have another piece. Then, he went and took a good, long nap. He had a habit of taking very long naps.

When he woke up, he finally started training. He began a highly regimented program that tested all of his endurance, speed, and flexibility. In the morning, as soon as he woke up, he would go for a 20-mile jog. For meals, he would eat exclusively protein shakes. In the afternoon, he would spend 5 hours each day lifting weights, and then would go for another 20-mile jog in the evening.

Soon, Dr. Hofbrincl became quite ripped, even though he still weighed quite a bit more than the average human being. Instead of playing video games, he would do pushups. Instead of taking long naps, he would do pushups. And instead of eating cake, he would do more pushups.

Finally, the day of the marathon came. The day he had been waiting for his whole life, even though he had decided to compete in the marathon only a month ago. He got in his car and drove to the marathon.

When he reached the start site, he could hardly control his excitement. That morning for breakfast, he had wolfed down 14 protein shakes, so he was filled with energy.

"I'm filled with energy!" he said as he ran up to the starting line, where the other contestants were standing. Many of them looked as if they had been training ever since they were born – and even though Dr. Hofbrincl had been preparing for the last month, he still weighed considerably more than the others.

"All right, everyone, gather around," said the announcer. "Thank you all for participating in today's marathon. Although as you may have noticed, this is not a traditional marathon."

Dr. Hofbrincl became a bit confused. He had been training for a normal marathon, the kind where you run for 26 miles.

Oh wait, he thought. *I'm sorry. I meant 42km. Gosh darn these metric units.*

Dr. Hofbrincl wanted to make sure that everything was all right and all of his effort was not for naught, so he asked the announcer, "Excuse me, sir, but if this is not a traditional marathon, what kind of marathon is it?"

"I'm glad you asked," said the announcer, even though he was clearly annoyed at the question. "Instead of being a normal marathon, this is the first ever Mass Spectromethon!"

"So what's the difference?" asked Dr. Hofbrincl.

"You'll see," said the announcer in an ominous tone of voice.

Dr. Hofbrincl noticed that it was getting to be quite hot outside. This was odd, because when he had previously checked the weather, it was supposed to have been quite chilly.

Then, he realized that all of the contestants were being sprayed by some sort of vapor coming from a machine on the side of the track. The machine, which had a logo saying "Vapor" on it, was showering all of the runners with steam.

This is quite odd, thought Dr. Hofbrincl. *Although I guess it's supposed to make all of the runners loosen up before the big race.*

The announcer began giving instructions to the contestants. "All right, the first thing I need everyone to do is wear one of these bracelets so we can easily identify you."

Dr. Hofbrincl rushed over the the side of the track, where they were handing out bracelets. As he put the bracelet on, he realized that it was made entirely out of iron.

"These are really heavy," he told his fellow marathon-runners. "I feel like it's going to weigh me down during the race."

"Shut up," they told him.

As Dr. Hofbrincl turned the bracelet over, he caught a logo inscribed on the bottom of the bracelet, which read "Ion."

That is a funny way to spell Iron, he thought. *No other marathon makes people wear metal bracelets. Oh, well. You win some, you lose some.*

"Shut up," the other contestants told him. It was then that Dr. Hofbrincl realized that he had been speaking out loud the whole time.

Once everyone had put on the Ion bracelets, the announcer issued the next set of instructions.

"I know that all of you are excited to get going, but in the past we have had an issue with people getting cramps, so we all want you to be properly warmed up beforehand," said the announcer.

Dr. Hofbrincl raised his hand. "I'm sorry, sir, but how did you have these issues in the past? I thought you said that this was the first ever Mass Spectromethon," he said.

"Shut up," said the announcer. "I didn't say you could speak."

"Oh all right, I'm sorry," said Dr. Hofbrincl.

"You're still talking, and I don't know why," said the announcer. Then, he stood up straight and raised the microphone to his mouth in a grand gesture.

"Everyone, get on the starting line. READY…SET…GO!" yelled the announcer.

Dr. Hofbrincl took off running. He had been preparing for this day for so long. He was wearing all of the latest sports gear – although for some reason, he was still wearing his usual lab coat.

He could feel his legs move in perfect runners' motion, pulsing back and forth. He felt like he was flying – he was traveling faster and faster until he could go no more. Soon, he got tired, but he somehow kept running, faster than he ever had before.

How is this possible? he thought. Then, he looked behind him, and he realized how he had been able to travel so fast. Behind all the runners was a huge fan, a giant machine that was blowing air towards the runners, making them run extremely fast. Dr. Hofbrincl noticed that there was a logo on the fan that looked like "Accelerate."

That's pretty cool, he thought. *This way, I don't even have to run, but I'll still finish the marathon.*

However, he soon began to realize that something was going terribly wrong. In the first part of the marathon, all of the runners were supposed to go forward in a straight line. However, some of the runners who were not as heavy as Dr. Hofbrincl were trailing off to the left.

"Wait! You can't run to the left! That's cheating!" he yelled at the runners.

"I'm sorry!" yelled back one of the runners. "It's not our fault. We're not trying to run left. It's these bracelets! They're pulling us away…"

"Oh dear!" exclaimed Dr. Hofbrincl. He wondered what could possibly be causing all of the bracelets to pull all the runners to the left. Although he noticed that he, as well as the other runners who were not very skinny, continued to go in a straight line.

He could feel his Ion bracelet pulling him to his left, but he kept his ground. Staring forward, he was determined to not be pulled to the left.

Unfortunately, not everyone had the will of Dr. Hofbrincl. Some of the other runners were pulled left, even thought they fought extremely hard.

Some of the bracelets of the younger runners who were just mere children were so powerful that they actually caused the kids to fly in the air towards the left.

As Dr. Hofbrincl looked to his left, he saw a huge machine labeled "Deflection."

That's odd, he thought. *Why are there so many machines in this marathon?*

This machine looked like a huge magnet, sucking in all of the runners. Every once in a while, the magnet would light up, and so would all of the bracelets. Each time this happened, the runners would be pulled towards the giant magnet on the left.

Dr. Hofbrincl noticed that the heavier the runner was, the less likely the runner was to be affected by the machine. The lighter runners tended to be pulled more towards the left by the magnet.

It's probably just a coincidence, thought Dr. Hofbrincl.

Finally, Dr. Hofbrincl saw the finish line. It was just ahead of him, with the label "Detection." He ran and ran and ran until his feet were killing him, and then he would just kind of stand there and be pushed forward by the giant fan for a while, and then he would continue running.

After what seemed like eternity, he ran past the finish line. He was finished! All of his long hours of hard work had paid off in the end!

"CONGRATULATIONS!" boomed the voice of the announcer. "You have all finished the first ever MASS SPECTROMETHON! I'm sorry I had to keep all of you waiting so long. Our last contestant, by the name of ... I believe, Dr. Hofbrincl...took quite a bit longer than the rest of you to finish the marathon."

"I'm sorry," said Dr. Hofbrincl, who was gasping for air and catching his breath. "I think this lab coat was slowing me down."

"I didn't say you could speak," said the announcer.

Then, the announcer finally unveiled what was going on.

"As you might have guessed, the Mass Spectromethon is not a normal marathon, but rather is structured like a Mass Spectrometer. Does anyone know what that is?"

Dr. Hofbrincl raised his hand, and the announcer called on him. At last, this was his chance to speak. "A mass spectrometer is a device used in Chemistry that can separate different molecules based on their masses."

"Good job!" exclaimed the announcer. "The Mass Spectrometer in this marathon was used to separate all of the contestants based on their masses as well. As you may have noticed, the more massive contestants like Dr. Hofbrincl traveled in a straight line, while the less massive contestants are now standing on the left."

One of the runners raised his hand. "That's really cool! How does a mass spectrometer work?" he asked.

Explanation

As you may have noticed, there were five different aspects of the machines in this race, which are the five different parts of a mass spectrometer. This is how they function:

1. Vaporization. This is the first step, which involves (you guessed it) vaporizing the substance you are working with. Basically, this involves heating it up so it becomes a gas. In the story, all of the contestants were heated up by the Vapor machine.

2. Ionization. This step shoots electrons at the vaporized substance, which has the effect of knocking off electrons from the substance. After ionization takes place, most of the particles in the substance now have a +1 positive charge because they have all lost electrons. In the story, the bracelets represent Ionization.

3. Acceleration. This step involves rapidly moving the substance through the mass spectrometer. This way, we are able to track the motion of the particles in the substance. In the story, the giant fan represents the accelerator.

4. Deflection. This is perhaps the most important part of the process. The mass spectrometer uses a magnet to deflect the particles in the machine. Because all of the particles have a +1 charge, they are affected by a magnetic field. However, due to the principle of inertia, the heavier particles are deflected less than the smaller particles. In the story, the giant magnet represents the deflector. The larger people were able to go in a straight line, but the lighter people were deflected more easily by the magnetic field acting on the bracelets.

5. Detection. When the particles reach the end of the machine, the mass spectrometer records where the particles hit. This way, we can measure how much the particles were deflected, and thus gauge their masses. In the story, the finish line represented the detector.

Chapter 5

FREE RADICAL REACTIONS

After finally finishing the Mass Spectromethon, Dr. Hofbrincl came to the fallacious conclusion that exercise was not really a necessary part of living. He felt that he had actually been happier before his massive exercise program. And although it was kind of cool to finish a race, he really didn't get anything out of it.

Therefore, he soon returned to his old approach to life: one of relaxation and idleness.

After taking a nice, long shower, he slipped into his pajamas and lied down on the couch. Then, he thought that he could make an important point about grammar. You are probably thinking it is better to say that he had laid down instead of lied down. However, according to the Merriam-Webster Dictionary, the word "lie" means "to be or to stay at rest in a horizontal position", whereas the word "lay" means "to put or set down."

Therefore, people can lie down, but they cannot lay down. However, they can lay themselves down, as that would indicate that they were placing themselves down.

So, Dr. Hofbrincl could either have lied down or laid himself down.

"Enough with all the grammar!" yelled Dr. Hofbrincl. "I'm trying to relax."

Clearly, Dr. Hofbrincl had no appreciation for the beauty of the English language. Instead of choosing to read a dictionary or thesaurus, he decided to lay down on his couch, grab the TV remote, and turn on the news.

I'm sorry, I meant "lie down," not "lay down." Whoops.

"I really don't care," said Dr. Hofbrincl, once again showing his disdain for linguistic prowess.

While lying on the couch, he reached for the remote and turned on his TV. The daily news channel was on again.

Gosh darn, he thought. *Why does my wife keep watching the daily news? I would much rather watch TV shows that don't have any educational value because I hate acquiring knowledge.*

Unfortunately, as he tried to change the channel, he realized that the TV remote batteries had just run out. But instead of changing them, he decided that that was a job for another time. And another person. Probably his wife. He decided he would try and slip it into conversation tonight at dinner, and hopefully she would take the hint.

"BREAKING NEWS!" exclaimed the TV announcer. "There has been a prison jailbreak! The infamous criminal named Free Radical has escaped from his life sentence in prison!"

Oh dear, this is terrible news! thought Dr. Hofbrincl. He remembered hearing about Free Radical. Apparently, Free Radical was a man who had been going around the country, stealing refrigerators. After many valiant citizens complained to the police about their food getting spoiled, the police finally caught him and put him in jail.

"For those of you who don't know," continued the announcer, "Free Radical was a man who had been going around the country, stealing refrigerators. After many valiant citizens complained to the police about their food getting spoiled, the police finally caught him and put him in jail."

Wow, this is kind of like Déjà vu, thought Dr. Hofbrincl. *Anyways, this doesn't concern me at all. Free Radical was arrested all the way across the country. It's not like he's going to come knocking at my doorstep all of a sudden and ask to see my refrigerator.*

Suddenly, Dr. Hofbrincl heard a knock on the door.

Knock, knock.

"Who's there?" shouted Dr. Hofbrincl.

"It's me, your wife!" said the person at the door.

"It's me, your wife, who?" asked Dr. Hofbrincl.

"Wait, what? No, it's actually your wife. This isn't a knock knock joke."

Dr. Hofbrincl approached the door and let his wife in. "By the way, that was a horrible punch line," he told her.

"It wasn't a joke," she replied. "I didn't even say 'Knock Knock.' I just knocked on the door."

"Well, it was a good try anyways," Dr. Hofbrincl said. He had always prided himself on his well-developed sense of humor. He considered it to be one of the few positive aspects about him. Others considered it to be a nuisance.

As soon as he closed the door, he heard another knock.

"Again, really? It's not even funny this time," said Dr. Hofbrincl.

"It's not me!" his wife exclaimed. "I'm already in the living room, and I'm pretty sure this isn't a joke!"

Dr. Hofbrincl sighed. Nobody seemed to understand him or get his sense of humor. Dejected, he opened the door and saw a young man standing in the doorway.

This man looked like he could be somewhat of a criminal. He was very lean, and looked like he had been in prison for quite some time. He wore a shirt that said "Free Radical" as well as a name tag that said "Hello, my name is Free Radical" on it.

"Hi, my name is Dr. Hofbrincl," said Dr. Hofbrincl. "How may I help you?"

The man, who looked a lot like the escaped convict Free Radical, began laughing uncontrollably.

"Wow, that joke was really good!" exclaimed the man.

"Why thank you," said Dr. Hofbrincl. Finally, a man who got his sense of humor. He liked this new guy.

"Would you like to come inside?" asked Dr. Hofbrincl.

"Of course!" said the man. "I just needed to use your restroom. I drank a lot of water earlier today."

Dr. Hofbrincl thought the matter over and decided that there was no harm in letting a young man, who slightly resembled an escaped criminal, use his bathroom.

"Well of course you can use my restroom!" said Dr. Hofbrincl. "You know what they say … one small bathroom for man, a giant toilet for mankind!"

"I'm pretty sure that nobody has ever said that, and it doesn't really make any sense," said the young man. "But thanks anyways."

Dr. Hofbrincl went back to the couch and laid himself down. It had been a stressful three minutes of social interaction, and he needed time to unwind. He closed his eyes and took a long nap.

Zzzzzzzzzz.

Zzzzzzzzzz.

Zzzzzzzzzz.

"Honey!"

Zzzzzzzzzz.

"Where's our refrigerator?!?"

Zzzzzzzzzz.

"All of the food is rotting!"

Zzzzzzzzzz.

"This means we can't have dinner!"

Dr. Hofbrincl shot up from his nap. "NO DINNER!" he shouted. "WHAT HAPPENED?"

"Well, dear, it appears as if our refrigerator is missing. Someone must have taken it. All of the food is still here – although it's starting to rot," explained Mrs. Hofbrincl.

Suddenly, Dr. Hofbrincl realized what had happened. While he was helping the young man go to the bathroom, Free Radical must have somehow managed to sneak into the kitchen and steal his refrigerator. It had never occurred to him that the young man was in fact Free Radical.

"Well, this leaves us with only one course of action," said Dr. Hofbrincl.

"That's right," said Mrs. Hofbrincl. "We must call the police and report this theft."

"Of course not," said Dr. Hofbrincl. "That's a horrible idea. We should instead steal someone else's refrigerator to replace our old one."

"Well, all right then," agreed Mrs. Hofbrincl.

Soon, Dr. Hofbrincl arranged a visit with his friend Alfred. While he was over at Alfred's house, he stole Alfred's refrigerator.

Alfred decided that since he was lacking a refrigerator, he would steal one from his friend Bert.

Bert, after losing his refrigerator to Alfred, stole one from Carl, who stole one from David, who stole one from Evan, who stole one from Frank, who stole one from George, who finally stole the refrigerator back from Dr. Hofbrincl.

Well, this is awkward, thought Dr. Hofbrincl. *After all of this, I still don't have a refrigerator.*

Finally, Mrs. Hofbrincl decided that it was time to intervene. "This has propagated long enough! It's time to terminate this madness!" she exclaimed.

Mrs. Hofbrincl finally called the police, who were eventually able to track down the criminal Free Radical and arrest him again, after following a trail of stolen refrigerators. And in the end, justice was restored.

"So I guess I've learned my lesson," said Dr. Hofbrincl.

"You've realized that stealing refrigerators from your friends is wrong?" asked Mrs. Hofbrincl.

"Of course not, silly," said Dr. Hofbrincl. "That was a great idea. In the future, I need to set up an alarm system around our refrigerator so that it will notify the police whenever an unauthorized person attempts to move it."

Explanation

This story attempted, probably unsuccessfully, to demonstrate how a free radical reaction works. A free radical is a type of molecule that has an unpaired valence electron (for example, it might have seven valence electrons instead of the usual eight). These types of molecules are very unstable, and will therefore try to bond with other molecules in order to have all of their electrons paired.

Free radical reactions have three steps: initiation, propagation, and termination.

Initiation refers to the formation of the free radical. In the story, the initiation was when Free Radical escaped from prison.

Propagation refers to how the free radical reacts with other molecules and turns them into free radicals. The propagation in the story is when Free Radical turns the others into unstable free radicals themselves. When he steals Dr. Hofbrincl's refrigerator, Dr. Hofbrincl becomes unstable because he is missing his refrigerator, which is analogous to an electron. Then, he steals Alfred's refrigerator, causing Alfred to become a free radical, and so on and so forth.

Termination refers to when all of the free radicals react with each other so that no more free radicals remain. In this story, Free Radical goes back to prison, which represents the reaction ending.

Chapter 6

CARBON HYBRIDIZATION

Dr. Hofbrincl began trying to set up a refrigerator alarm system, but quickly gave up after a couple of minutes after realizing that it was quite difficult to do so. Therefore, he went back to his couch and took a nap instead.

When he woke up, he decided to watch one of his favorite movies: *The Pink Panther*, starring Steve Martin. He thought of himself as a very similar character to Jacques Clouseau. However, when he turned on Netflix, he realized that his subscription had expired.

This is odd, he thought. *Why am I suddenly unable to Netflix and Chill?*

Since contemplating the reasons for this dilemma required thinking, and thinking was hard, he decided that he would instead go to the neighborhood store and buy a copy of *The Pink Panther* himself.

With a burst of energy, Dr. Hofbrincl stood up and got off the couch.

Wow, what a head rush! he thought.

He grabbed his keys and went to his garage. He put the keys in the ignition and turned the keys, but nothing happened. Then, he realized that he had sold his car a couple of days ago to pay for rent, and that he was actually just shoving a carrot into a garbage can.

Whoops, he thought. *Rookie mistake.*

Since he didn't have a car, his only option was to walk to the store.

Oh, no! he thought. *I hate walking.*

Unfortunately, he had no choice. Dr. Hofbrincl went back into his house, chugged a protein shake, and then walked to the store.

After what seemed like eternity, he finally arrived at the door of the store. Although he was completely out of breath, he managed to open the door just wide enough for him to slip in.

"Someone help me!" he gasped. "QUICK!"

One of the cashiers rushed over to him. "What do you need, sir?" she asked.

"I need a copy of the movie *The Pink Panther*," he said.

"Oh, alright," she said. "Just wait here a moment, and I'll be right back with it."

Dr. Hofbrincl waited for a moment, and then the cashier came right back, this time holding a DVD of *The Pink Panther*.

"DVD!" Dr. Hofbrincl exclaimed. "I thought that this was the age of Blu-Ray discs!"

"Oh, alright," she said. "Just wait here a moment, and I'll be right back with it."

Dr. Hofbrincl waited for a moment, and then the cashier came right back, this time holding a Blu-Ray disc of *The Pink Panther*.

"Why thank you," said Dr. Hofbrincl as he reached into his pocket to pull out his wallet. He handed his credit card to the cashier to pay for the movie.

The cashier smiled at Dr. Hofbrincl and ran the credit card through the card reader. Then, she slowly raised one eyebrow and handed the card back.

"I'm sorry, sir, but our machine is rejecting this credit card. Apparently you don't have any money."

"This must be a mistake," said Dr. Hofbrincl, as he handed her another card.

The cashier smiled at Dr. Hofbrincl and ran the new credit card through the card reader. Then, she slowly raised one eyebrow and handed the card back.

"I'm sorry, sir, but our machine is rejecting this credit card as well. Apparently you don't have any money."

"Well, this is no bueno," said Dr. Hofbrincl, using this opportunity to practice the Spanish that he had learned in middle school. "Claro que sí no hubiera tenido refresco pollo loco."

"I'm sorry, but I don't speak Spanish," said the cashier.

"Neither do I," said Dr. Hofbrincl. "I was just spewing gibberish for no reason."

"Oh, how wonderful. Now are you paying for the movie or not?"

Dr. Hofbrincl was at somewhat of a crossroads, an impasse if you will. He was shocked that he didn't have enough money to pay for the movie. He thought that the purpose of credit cards was that payment was not necessary. So to resolve this problem, he turned to the one person who he knew could solve this situation: his wife.

He pulled out his phone and dialed her number. However, since he had not paid his phone bill, he couldn't complete the call. So he used the cashier's phone instead.

Ring, ring.

Dr. Hofbrincl waited for his wife to pick up the phone.

Ring, ring.

While he waited, Dr. Hofbrincl appreciated the use of onomatopoeia in describing the phone call.

Ring, ring.

"Hello?"

"Hi, this is Dr. Hofbrincl," said Dr. Hofbrincl. "Why do I have no money?"

"I'm not exactly sure, honey," said Mrs. Hofbrincl. "Maybe it's because you haven't gone to your job in four months?"

"What an astute observation!" exclaimed Dr. Hofbrincl in awe. He never would have thought of that. "What should I do?"

"Well, for one thing, you could go back to your job and work for a change," she advised.

"How clever!" he said. He would never have thought of doing that either.

After hanging up and returning the phone to the cashier, he walked to his office building. Although it seemed like he was walking a lot, the store was next door, and his office building was just across the street. So perhaps a total of 2 minutes walking.

As he walked through the front doors, he saw all of his coworkers arranged in a circle. As they saw him walk in, their faces lit up in excitement.

"Dr. Hofbrincl, you're back! We were beginning to get worried!"

"It's so great to see you again!"

"Nice haircut!"

Dr. Hofbrincl was thrilled. He hadn't gotten a haircut recently due to his monetary difficulties, but he was glad somebody liked his hair.

"So what's going on?" asked Dr. Hofbrincl.

"Well," said his boss, whose name was James. "Today is a company retreat day, but instead of going to a far off place, we're just going to do it in our boring, mundane, ennui-inducing office building."

"That's a great idea!" exclaimed Dr. Hofbrincl. "So James, what are we doing in the retreat?"

"We're going to do a couple of exercises to strengthen our workers' bonds," said James. "But before we begin, you should meet our new intern."

A young man wearing a suit studded with diamonds and graphite stepped forward and shook Dr. Hofbrincl's hand.

"Hi, my name is Carbon," he said. "But everyone calls me 'The Building Block of Life,' or 'BBOL' for short."

"It's nice to meet you," said Dr. Hofbrincl. He was immediately jealous of this new intern. He had always wanted a cool nickname. The only one he had had so far in his life was 'Plaintiff,' and that too only for a couple of weeks.

However, he noticed something a bit off about this new intern. There was something weird about his hands … and as he looked more closely, his feet.

This is weird, he thought. *Something eerie is going on.*

Then, Dr. Hofbrincl realized what had happened. Instead of having two hands and two feet, BBOL had four limbs that were almost identical.

Dr. Hofbrincl also noticed that BBOL had a tattoo on his neck that said SP3.

Wow, this guy is really cool and mysterious, he thought. *I wish I could have a tattoo and a mixture of feet and hands.*

"All right, everyone gather around," said James. "Our first exercise is designed to increase interconnectedness. You have four limbs each, so our first exercise is to have all of your limbs connected to someone else's. Alright … GO!"

Dr. Hofbrincl desperately looked around for people's hands to grab. Since James was right next to him, he grabbed one of James' hands with his right hand. He felt two people grab his feet, which meant that his left hand was the only limb left that he had to grab someone's limb with.

Wow, I love my company, he thought. *What is my job again?*

At that precise moment, he felt someone grab his other arm. That meant that for the purposes of this exercise, he had done his job. As he looked to his left, he realized that the person who had grabbed his other hand was BBOL.

What great teamwork, he thought. *I'm starting to like BBOL.*

However, once everyone else had gotten all of their limbs connected, he realized that there was a slight problem. For some reason that was actually mathematically impossible, BBOL still had one limb left that wasn't grabbing anyone else's limb.

"Oh, no, this is terrible!" shouted Dr. Hofbrincl. Now there's no way we can finish the exercise!"

"Wait," said BBOL. "There's one thing we can do. Just watch and see."

Dr. Hofbrincl was intrigued. How could BBOL solve this problem?

BBOL took his free limb and slowly moved it up so that it touched his tattoo, which had previously said SP3. However, when he pressed on the tattoo and released his hand, the tattoo changed so that it said SP2 instead.

"Whoa!" exclaimed Dr. Hofbrincl. "How did you do that?"

"I'm not finished yet," said BBOL. "Just wait and see."

Suddenly, there was a flash of light. Dr. Hofbrincl was temporarily blinded. But when his vision started working again, he saw that BBOL, instead of having four limbs … now only had three.

"That's awesome!" Dr. Hofbrincl exclaimed. "Now we've finished the exercise!"

"Not quite," said James, the boss. "There's a slight problem in your formation. Both Dr. Hofbrincl and BBOL are grabbing the same person with one of their limbs."

As Dr. Hofbrincl looked around, he saw that James was right, as he usually was in these situations. Both he and BBOL were grabbing the same person, which was against the rules.

"NOOOOOOOO!" shouted Dr. Hofbrincl. "WHAT AM I GOING TO DOOOOO?"

"Don't worry about it," said BBOL with a smile on his face. With the limb that had been grabbing the person Dr. Hofbrincl was grabbing, he reached up to his neck and pressed his SP2 tattoo again.

There was another big flash of light. The SP2 tattoo had changed to only say SP, and BBOL now only had two limbs.

"That's super cool!" shouted Dr. Hofbrincl. "I wish I could do that."

BBOL winked at Dr. Hofbrincl. "I'm just a metaphor for the element carbon, not a real person."

"What?" asked Dr. Hofbrincl.

"Nothing," said BBOL.

"Congratulations!" exclaimed James. "You've all bonded well today. You can now collect your paychecks and go home."

Dr. Hofbrincl was tired after a long day of strenuous work. He collected his pay check, went to the store to buy *The Pink Panther*, then went home and took a long nap on his couch.

Explanation

This story is a metaphor for how the element carbon uses different hybridized orbitals in order to create bonds.

Hybridization refers to a blending of orbitals, and an orbital is a region of space where an electron is likely to be found. In order for carbon to bond with other atoms, it must share electrons with the other atoms.

Under the traditional model of the atom, carbon should only be allowed to make two bonds because it would have two electrons in the s-orbital, and two electrons in two of the three p-orbitals.

The reason for this is that electrons tend to fill up the lowest energy levels first, and then the higher ones later. The s-orbital is the lowest energy level, and it can hold two electrons. Once those are filled up, the electrons then go and fill up the p-orbitals. Because the s-orbital is filled up with the two electrons, it should not be able to form any bonds. Therefore, only the two electrons in the p-orbitals should be able to form bonds.

However, you may have noticed that carbon usually forms four bonds instead of two. It does this by 'hybridizing' the orbitals to change one s-orbital and three p-orbitals into four of the same type of orbital, called SP3 (because they consist of one s-orbital and three p-orbitals). In the story, the orbitals are represented by different limbs. When Dr. Hofbrincl observes that BBOL has four limbs that don't look like either hands or feet, that depicts the blending of the orbitals.

When carbon has three bonds (represented by BBOL having three limbs), it forms three SP2 orbitals, which are formed from one s-orbital and two p-orbitals. Since carbon has four valence electrons and only three of them are being used in the SP2 orbitals, the other electron is not used for bonding, and is instead 'delocalized,' meaning that it kind of hovers above and below the bonds, making them slightly stronger.

When carbon has two bonds (represented at the end when BBOL only has two limbs), it forms two SP orbitals, which are a combination of one s-orbital and one p-orbital. Since only two of the four electrons are used in the SP orbitals, the other two electrons become delocalized, meaning that they hover around the bonds, making them stronger.

Key Points

Although much of this is quite complicated and probably explained quite poorly, the important takeaway is that carbon can form two, three, or four bonds. When it changes the amount of bonds it can form, it hybridizes the orbitals, meaning that it blends the s-orbitals and p-orbitals to make it easier to form bonds.

Chapter 7

ERROR

*Note: This is not a mistake. The title of the chapter is "Error."

**Note: However, naming the chapter "Error" may have been an error, because it is not really about error.

When Dr. Hofbrincl woke up from his nap, he turned on his TV and began watching *The Pink Panther*. He loved how the movie was a real-life documentary of an extremely clever detective who ingeniously solved the crime of the theft of the Pink Panther diamond.

While Dr. Hofbrincl watched the movie, he ate a lot of popcorn, which helped offset the weight loss that had occurred during his marathon training. Similar to how some people play drinking games, Dr. Hofbrincl decided to play a popcorn-eating game – every time someone would say a word, he would eat a kernel of popcorn.

When the movie was over, Dr. Hofbrincl found himself at an impasse, or a crossroads if you will. He didn't know what to do next. He had already tried working at his job, but that had become kind of boring. He could have taken another nap, but he decided that he had slept so much over the past couple of days that were he to sleep more, it could have extremely dangerous health effects. Perhaps even fatal.

As Dr. Hofbrincl sat around doing nothing as usual, he was suddenly struck with an idea.

"Eureka!" he shouted, even though he was as usual, alone. "I've got it. I'm going to go on a … scavenger hunt!"

Dr. Hofbrincl had always been a huge fan of scavenger hunts. Ever since he had been a small child, he loved the thrill of finally reaching a destination, whether it be finding the treasure or writing the last chapter of a book.

Therefore, he got his phone book and tried to look up the number for an organization that conducted scavenger hunts. Then, he slowly realized that this was the 21st Century, and that phone books were no longer a thing. So he went online and Googled "scavenger hunt company" and got a phone number from there.

He picked up his phone and dialed the number. As he held the phone to his ear, he remembered that he had still not paid the phone bill – the only thing he had bought with his paycheck was the movie *The Pink Panther*.

"Mrs. Hofbrincl!" he called out to his wife, for some reason addressing her by her last name. "Have you paid the phone bill!"

"Of course!" she shouted back at him. "I paid it this morning. I was able to do that because I actually have a job and get money, which is able to support both of us. You should try to be more appreciative of that."

"Meh," he replied. He had stopped listening after she said "Of course!" As the phone rang, he could feel his heart beating with excitement. Although it may have been cholesterol.

Finally, the person on the other side of the line picked up.

"Hi, welcome to Uncertainty Scavenger Hunts, where we are always uncertain about what exactly we're doing. How can I help you?" said the voice.

"Um...I'd like to go on a scavenger hunt at some point today," said Dr. Hofbrincl.

"Wonderful!" exclaimed the voice. "Does today at 3 o'clock work?"

Dr. Hofbrincl checked his calendar. Today was empty. So was every other day.

"Yeah, that works."

"Great! Just show up today at 3 o'clock, and we'll sort it out from there," said the voice.

"My car is out of gas," said Dr. Hofbrincl. But the other person had already hung up.

Well, you win some, you lose some, he thought to himself.

He spent the whole day in anticipation.

"I can't wait for the scavenger hunt!" he exclaimed to Mrs. Hofbrincl.

"Shouldn't you be at your job?"

"Never mind," said Dr. Hofbrincl. He was supposed to be in the scavenger hunt office in an hour, so he figured that he would leave in fifty minutes. He then remembered that his car didn't work, so he left the house immediately and began walking.

After what seemed like days, Dr. Hofbrincl reached Uncertainty Scavenger Hunts. He opened the door and walked in.

"Hi, I'm here for my scavenger hunt," said Dr. Hofbrincl.

Seeing that nobody was in the room, he rang the bell on the front desk and waited for somebody to walk into the room. After a couple of minutes, somebody walked into the room.

"Hi, I'm here for my scavenger hunt," said Dr. Hofbrincl.

"Wonderful!" said the representative. "Let's begin. This is somewhat of an unorthodox scavenger hunt. Here, instead of having a bunch of steps you need to complete, we just challenge you to reach a destination."

This was good news for Dr. Hofbrincl. He hated taking many steps to do something – that's why he intensely disliked walking.

The representative continued. "Essentially, the goal of this scavenger hunt is to make you go to Kansas."

Dr. Hofbrincl asked a clarification question. "So basically, I'm paying you a bunch of money to go to Kansas, and if I reach Kansas, I win?"

"Exactly. That'll be $10,000."

Dr. Hofbrincl handed the representative his wife's credit card. She had a very well-paying job, and could stand to lose some money.

"This sounds so exciting!" exclaimed Dr. Hofbrincl. "What do I get if I win?"

"It's not about the destination, it's about the journey," said the representative.

Wow, such wise words, thought Dr. Hofbrincl. He resolved to keep that statement in mind, which may have been a bad decision, given that he was quite prone to forget things easily.

Dr. Hofbrincl left the scavenger hunt office and got ready to travel to Kansas. He had left his wife's credit card in the office, but he didn't want to delay his journey by going back to get it.

Usually, when people try to reach a destination that is far away, they tend to fly or drive. However, none of this occurred to Dr. Hofbrincl. He decided that instead, he would walk all the way to Kansas.

Usually, when people try to walk to a destination that is far away, they tend to either use a GPS or look up directions. However, none of this occurred to Dr.

Hofbrincl. He decided that instead, he would simply navigate to Kansas based on street signs.

What an effective method of going to Kansas! he thought. *I should teach people how to navigate more often.*

Dr. Hofbrincl began walking to Kansas. He vowed that he would not eat, he would not sleep, and he would not rest until he had reached Kansas. He began to feel like how he had felt before the marathon – excited, yet hungry.

After what seemed like months (because they were actually months), Dr. Hofbrincl finally arrived at his destination.

I'm finally here! he thought.

As he looked over the view of Kansas, he admired how beautiful the sun looked as it glinted off the Golden Gate Bridge.

Wait...what? he thought. *There's no Golden Gate Bridge in Kansas.*

Stricken with fear, Dr. Hofbrincl rushed to the nearest person he could find.

"Please, help me! What state are we in?" he asked.

"Goo goo ga ga," replied the person. As it turned out, the person was a baby.

Then, Dr. Hofbrincl turned to the baby's mother and asked the question again.

"This is clearly California," she said.

Dr. Hofbrincl was heartbroken. He was nowhere near Kansas. He once again began his trek through the wilderness of the USA in order to find the elusive Kansas.

Days passed. Weeks. Then months. And according to his broken watch, a couple of years. Finally, Dr. Hofbrincl arrived at his destination.

"Yes, I'm finally here!" he shouted. He looked out over the vast expanse of Kansas. He loved the view – especially the sun glinting off the Hollywood sign.

"Gosh darn!" he shouted. Once again, he was clearly in California.

Dr. Hofbrincl had had enough of this madness. He picked up his phone and called the Uncertainty Scavenger Hunt company.

"Hello, how can we help you?" asked the voice at the other end.

"I took part in your scavenger hunt and it told me to go to Kansas, but for some reason, every time I try to go to Kansas, I end up in California."

"Well, that's probably a bit awkward for you. Although you shouldn't be too hard on yourself. At least you're consistent. Some might even say ... precise," said the voice.

Precise? That sounded like a good thing to be. Suddenly, Dr. Hofbrincl was rejuvenated. A random stranger had said that he was precise! Although he didn't really know what that word meant, he resolved to finish this scavenger hunt once and for all.

"I'm going to finish this scavenger hunt!" he exclaimed to all of the people surrounding him.

"Goo goo ga ga," they replied. As he looked around, he realized that he was surrounded by a bunch of babies.

"Never mind," he said. "You'll all understand when you're older."

Dr. Hofbrincl, this time guided by the knowledge that he was precise (whatever that meant), began walking with a new conviction, a new determination to accomplish his goals. Although by now he had not eaten for about two years and his wife was extremely worried about his whereabouts, he remained focused on his goal of going to Kansas.

Finally, he reached his goal. As he looked out over the vast expanse of Kansas, he admired all of the sights that he could see – the Statue of Liberty, Times Square, and the Empire State Building.

Wait, he thought. *I'm not in Kansas. This is New York.*

Dr. Hofbrincl realized that all of his work was for nothing. He had literally wasted nearly three years of his life and had nothing to show for it.

He angrily dialed the number for the Uncertainty Scavenger Hunt office, hoping that his wife still worked and paid the phone bill.

"Hi, how can we help you?"

"I began this scavenger hunt three years ago, and I still haven't finished!" Dr. Hofbrincl yelled. "You've literally ruined my life! I'm stuck in New York!"

"Well, I think you're being a bit hard on yourself. You may not have reached the goal, but at least you're accurate," said the voice.

Accurate? thought Dr. Hofbrincl. *That sounds like a good thing to be. But how can I be accurate if I'm in New York, and my destination is Kansas?*

Then, he actually asked the question.

"How can I be accurate if I'm in New York, and my destination is Kansas?" he asked.

"Well, you landed in California and then New York. So if you go halfway in between, you're basically in Kansas."

"I guess that makes sense," said Dr. Hofbrincl. So in a way, he had achieved his goal. Dr. Hofbrincl was satisfied with this result, and also very hungry. Therefore, he went to a nearby McDonald's and ordered a Big Mac, thus making up for all of the Calories he should have eaten in the last three years.

What an eventful three years, he thought. Then, he went back to his house, reassured a frantic Mrs.

Hofbrincl that everything was all right, and took a long nap.

Explanation

This chapter was supposed to describe the difference between precision and accuracy. In science, precision means consistently achieving the same result, and accuracy means achieving the correct result.

Initially, Dr. Hofbrincl had precision, meaning that he obtained the same result over and over again. When he tried to find Kansas, he consistently ended up in California. In chemistry, it is important to conduct experiments with a high degree of precision because it shows that your experiment is repeatable and that you are not achieving the correct result by mere fluke.

However, Dr. Hofbrincl later had accuracy, which means that on average, he got the correct result. He ended up in California and then New York. If you take the spot of land in the middle of the two states, you end up somewhere near Kansas. Therefore, because the average of the results is the correct value, this is an accurate measurement. In chemistry, it is important to have a high degree of accuracy in order to ensure that the conclusions you draw from the data are valid and not arbitrary.

ABOUT THE AUTHOR

Bhavish Dinakar is currently a senior at Shawnee Mission East High School. His hobbies include playing the violin, performing card magic, composing jazz music, playing tennis, running his school's Knee Hockey club, attempting the synthesis of elusive chemical compounds, and computer programming.